Don't miss more fun adventures
with **Mindy Kim**!

Mindy Kim and the
Summer Musical

Mindy Kim

and the
Summer Musical

BOOK
9

By Lyla Lee
Illustrated by Dung Ho

ALADDIN
New York London Toronto Sydney New Delhi

❦ ALADDIN
An imprint of Simon & Schuster Children's Publishing Division
1230 Avenue of the Americas, New York, New York 10020
First Aladdin hardcover edition July 2023
Text copyright © 2023 by Lyla Lee
Illustrations copyright © 2023 by Dung Ho
Also available in an Aladdin paperback edition.
All rights reserved, including the right of reproduction in whole or in part in any form.
ALADDIN and related logo are registered trademarks of Simon & Schuster, Inc.
For information about special discounts for bulk purchases, please contact Simon & Schuster Special Sales at 1-866-506-1949 or business@simonandschuster.com.
The Simon & Schuster Speakers Bureau can bring authors to your live event. For more information or to book an event contact the Simon & Schuster Speakers Bureau at 1-866-248-3049 or visit our website at www.simonspeakers.com.
Designed by Laura Lyn DiSiena
The illustrations for this book were rendered digitally.
The text of this book was set in Haboro.
Manufactured in the United States of America 0523 FFG
10 9 8 7 6 5 4 3 2 1
Library of Congress Cataloging-in-Publication Data
Names: Lee, Lyla, author. | Ho, Dung, illustrator.
Title: Mindy Kim and the summer musical / by Lyla Lee ; illustrated by Dung Ho.
Description: First Aladdin paperback edition. | New York : Aladdin, 2023. |
Series: Mindy Kim ; book 9 | Audience: Ages 6 to 9. | Summary: Mindy tries to step into the spotlight in her community theater production.
Identifiers: LCCN 2022046640 (print) | LCCN 2022046641 (ebook) | ISBN 9781665935760 (hardcover) | ISBN 9781665935753 (paperback) | ISBN 9781665935777 (ebook)
Subjects: CYAC: Musicals–Fiction. | Korean Americans–Fiction.
Classification: LCC PZ7.1.L419 Mij 2023 (print) | LCC PZ7.1.L419 (ebook) | DDC [Fic]–dc23
LC record available at https://lccn.loc.gov/2022046640
LC ebook record available at https://lccn.loc.gov/2022046641

To all the readers out there who
made another year of Mindy books possible.
Thank you! <3

Chapter 1

My name is Mindy Kim. It's finally summer, and my best friend, Sally, and I have really fun plans. We're going to try out for a musical at our local community theater!

"I'm so glad you want to audition with me this year," Sally said with a wide grin. "I've always wanted to, but I was too afraid to try out by myself."

The two of us were lying on her bed, staring down at Sally's phone screen. She'd pulled up information about the summer musical, which was going to be *Cinderella* this year!

I wanted to go to Key West this summer, but Dad

said we can't afford to go yet. So I was glad that I could still have a fun vacation at home with Sally.

"Of course!" I replied. "I've never tried out for a play before, and I want to give it a shot."

The truth is, I was kind of scared too. Even though I ran for class president and tried my best to get over my fears, talking in front of a lot of people still makes me feel a little nervous. And singing and dancing in front of a crowd is probably a lot harder, so much so that it even scares Sally!

"When my sisters were in the musical a few years ago, they did *Alice in Wonderland*," Sally continued. "It was so fun! I'm sure this year's play will be awesome too."

She tapped her feet in excitement before getting up from her bed. When she turned to look at me, I tried my best to smile. I must have not done a very good job of it, though, because Sally frowned. "Hey, are you sure you want to audition for the musical with me? We don't have to if you don't want to!"

I shook my head. "I do! I'm just nervous about performing in front of a lot of people. And about the audition."

I've sung plenty in front of Theodore the Mutt, my dog, and played pretend with him and my stuffed animals all the time. But not in front of real-life people!

Sally sat back on the edge of her bed with a sigh.

"I think it's normal to feel that way when we're about to do something new!" Sally said. "But it's okay—we'll have each other! I don't know about you, but for me, just having you there with me will *definitely* help a lot."

I nodded. That was exactly what I thought too!

Suddenly I got an idea.

"What if we ask another friend to join us?" I suggested to Sally. "Then we'll be even less nervous!"

Sally smiled. She looked just as excited as I was. "That's a great idea! Do you know anyone else who might be interested in trying out for the musical with us?"

I thought for a moment. "Do you remember Lindsey? She was in our class in third grade, and I was in the same swim class with her when I was still learning how to swim."

"The girl who said she had a pony in Minnesota? I remember her!"

"Yeah! She's really nice. I can ask her if she wants to join."

"Sure! The more the merrier!"

I really hoped Lindsey could audition with us too. I crossed my fingers as we called her on Sally's phone.

Chapter 2

A musical? Sounds amazing!" Lindsey said when we told her about our plans. "I've only sung during karaoke with my mom and grandma, though. They always say that I'm a good singer, but they might just be saying that to be nice."

Sally and I laughed.

"It's okay," I said. "I think we're all nervous about singing in front of lots of people. It's going to be a new experience for all of us!"

When I went back home for dinner, Theodore greeted me at the door, his ears back and his tail wagging in circles like a helicopter.

"Hey, boy, where's Julie and Dad?" I asked him. Their cars were in the driveway, so I knew they were home.

Like always, Theodore didn't say anything back, but he didn't need to, because at that moment I heard Julie's and Dad's voices coming from the dining room.

"I'm sure she'll take the news well," Dad said. "I'm so excited to finally tell her. Are you?"

"I am," replied Julie, her voice softer than usual. "And I hope you're right."

"Tell me what?" I asked as I entered the kitchen.

Dad and Julie startled and quickly got up from the table. They both had weird looks on their faces! They were smiling, but they looked scared, too.

"Is everything okay?" I added when neither of them answered.

Dad and Julie looked at each other. Julie gave Dad a small nod, and Dad said, "Mindy, we have something very important to tell you. We wanted to wait until things were more . . . certain before we did, which is why we didn't say anything until now."

I bit my lip. I wished he would just tell me what was going on already!

"Do you remember how, when you were little, you said you wanted a sibling?" Dad continued. "You even asked Santa Claus for a little sister one year, back when we used to live in California."

I gasped, covering my mouth with my hands. I turned to Julie and asked, "Are you *pregnant*?"

Julie smiled and nodded. "I am." She bit her lip and continued, "How does that make you feel, Mindy?"

I dropped my hands so Julie could see the big smile on my face. My heart was beating so fast, like it was about to burst. "I'm so happy! Congratulations, Julie! Congratulations, Appa!"

I held out my arms wide so I could hug them. Dad and Julie wrapped their arms around me, holding me tight.

"I'm so glad you're happy, Mindy," Julie said. "I wasn't sure how you were going to take the news. Your dad said you'd like it, but I was still nervous. It's going to be a big change for all of us!"

They both gave me forehead kisses, and Dad said, "You're going to be a big sister, Mindy! And I can't think of another kid who is better suited for the job. You're gonna be great."

I let out an uneasy laugh. I hoped Dad was right! Even though I was for sure happy about getting a sibling, I was less sure about being an older sister. What if I wasn't grown-up or nice enough to be a good one?

"I hope so!" I said, squeezing Dad's and Julie's hands. "I'll try my hardest to be the best big sister I can be!"

Chapter 3

During dinner, I told Dad and Julie that I was trying out for the summer musical.

Dad clapped his hands.

"That sounds like a fantastic idea, Mindy!" he said. "What a great way to get out of your comfort zone."

"A fun one, too!" Julie added. "I've heard amazing things about the children's musical at the community theater. Everyone seems to enjoy it a lot!"

That weekend, the three of us went to the theater. There was an important meeting for the parents and kids so we could learn more about the musical. We arrived early, but the building was already crowded with lots of people. A few of the kids were from my school, but I didn't recognize the rest.

Seeing everyone there made me nervous. How were Sally, Lindsey, *and* I supposed to get roles when there were so many people trying out for the same spots?

Julie, Dad, and I sat next to Sally and Lindsey. Sally was there with her parents, while Lindsey was there with her mom and grandma.

When we were settled, people passed us thick packets of colorful paper.

"Hello, everyone!" said the lady onstage. She had short purple hair and red horn-rimmed glasses. "My name is Maria Kamper. I'm the children's musical director here at Sunshine County Community Theater. We are so excited by this huge turnout! In the packets you received or will receive, you will find information about this summer's musical, *Cinderella*. The information is also available on our website."

We looked through the packets together. They had all kinds of information, from when the audition was—in two weeks—to what we would wear for the official show day—costumes that we would get from the theater.

"There is a cast of fifteen main characters, with twenty-five other kids making up the ensemble," Ms. Kamper continued. "Due to theater capacity, we can only accept forty kids total. If you don't make it this time, we strongly encourage you to try again next year!"

My friends and I looked nervously at one another. There were definitely a lot more than forty kids sitting in the audience right now.

After the information session, Julie asked us, "So, girls, which role do you want to play?"

"I want to be Cinderella!" Sally said. "It's probably going to be the hardest role, so I'm going to try my best!"

"Same here!" Lindsey said. "The costume for

Cinderella looks so cute. I've always wanted to be a princess!"

"I want to be Cinderella too," I admitted in a quiet voice.

The three of us all stared at one another in surprise. Competition was fierce already!

The adults laughed.

"Well, it looks like you girls are going to have to compete against one another!" Dad said. "Try your best, but if you don't make it, remember, there are plenty of other roles too."

We nodded and nervously smiled at one another.

I wasn't sure who else I would want to be, other than Cinderella, but I really hoped we would all make it into the play!

Chapter 4

For the next two weeks, Lindsey, Sally, and I practiced for the audition. We had to memorize an entire song and read a scene from the play. It was hard work. I chose to sing "Somewhere Over the Rainbow" from *The Wizard of Oz*, one of my favorites. It was a pretty song, but boy, was it challenging to learn!

Thankfully, Sally was right: having friends to cheer me on as I practiced made everything a lot more fun. On some days we practiced at Sally's house, while on others we went to Lindsey's or mine. The best part was being able to play with each other's dogs during breaks and munch on snacks together when we got hungry!

When I wasn't practicing with my friends, I also rehearsed in front of Dad, Julie, and Theodore. It was a whole family effort! One time, just for fun, we even cast Theodore as the prince and made him a little crown out of yellow construction paper. In almost no time at all, he tore it up into little pieces. He's lucky he's cute!

And then, finally, it was time for the audition.

When we got to the community theater, Ms. Kamper handed my friends and me pieces of paper that told us what place we were in line. Of the three of us, Lindsey was going first, then Sally, and finally, me! My hands felt sweaty. I wished I weren't going last among my friends!

We sat with our families in the audience so we could watch a few of the other auditions before ours. Some people had already tried out yesterday, so there weren't as many people as there were at the meeting. My friends and I held one another's hands tightly as we waited for our turns.

Some of the kids who auditioned before us were good, while others weren't so great. One kid even threw up in the middle of his audition!

Dad winced as Ms. Kamper escorted the boy off the stage and someone came to clean up. "Poor kid," he said.

When it was Lindsey's turn, she squeezed both Sally's and my hands before she went up onto the stage.

"You can do it!" I yelled.

"Go, Lindsey!" said Sally.

Lindsey looked nervous, and I got sweaty again just by watching her. I could hear my own heartbeat, which went like *BA-DUM, BA-DUM, BA-DUM*!

Lindsey took a deep breath and started singing. The moment she did, I let out a sigh of relief. She sang so well! By the time Lindsey was done, Ms. Kamper even had tears in her eyes.

"Bravo!" she said, giving Lindsey a standing ovation. "Well done!"

Lindsey did great with the scene reading part of the audition too. From Ms. Kamper's reactions, I was sure she was going to make it into the play!

I high-fived Lindsey when she came back to her seat. "Great job!"

"Thanks!" she replied. "Whew, I was nervous, but I'm glad I was able to make it through the entire audition."

"You were fantastic!" Sally replied. "One down, two to go."

A few other kids went after Lindsey. They were all pretty good. And then it was Sally's turn. Sally didn't look as nervous as Lindsey did, or at least she didn't seem like it at first. But when she reached the stage, she tripped!

We all gasped.

Sally looked like she was about to cry, so I cupped my mouth with my hands and said, "You can do it, Sally!" Our families all joined in, shouting encouraging things at her.

She bit her lip but continued with her audition. Her voice wobbled a little, but she made it all the way through too.

"Yay!" We all cheered for Sally when she came back to her seat.

A couple more kids went after Sally, and then it was finally my turn.

Shaking from head to toe, I headed to the stage.

Chapter 5

If I thought running for class president was scary, that was nothing compared to standing onstage in front of so many people!

The stage lights were so bright and hot around me. Sweat beaded on my forehead. I clutched the microphone tightly in my hands. It almost slid out because of how sweaty my hands were!

BA-DUM! BA-DUM! BA-DUM! My heart was beating loudly again, but this time it was a lot faster than before.

I looked out into the audience. I could dimly make out Dad, Julie, and my friends in their seats.

Sally cupped her hands around her mouth and said, "You can do it, Mindy!"

"Yeah!" exclaimed Lindsey. "You're going to do great!"

"Mindy Kim?" said Ms. Kamper. "You're auditioning for the role of Cinderella, correct? What song are you going to be singing for us today?"

BA-DUM! BA-DUM! BA-DUM!

"'Somewhere Over the Rainbow' from *The Wizard of Oz*," I said. My voice came out quiet and shaky! I'd practiced so hard for the audition, but now I wasn't sure if I could even sing. My head felt all fuzzy, too. I hoped I could still remember how the song went!

I squeezed my eyes shut and tried to take deep, slow breaths. It's something Julie taught me to do whenever I get nervous!

"Whenever you're ready," Ms. Kamper said.

When I opened my eyes again, everything was a lot less bright.

"I'm ready," I said.

Ms. Kamper started playing piano, and even though I could barely hear myself over my own heartbeat, I still came in when I was supposed to. It was like my body remembered how to sing the song all on its own.

Dad whistled, and everyone else cheered some more. They sounded far, far away, like they were at the other end of a tunnel. But they still made me smile. I felt a lot more confident than I had before!

Then, finally, the song was over.

"Fantastic job!" said Ms. Kamper. "Now let's see you read some lines from the script."

I started reading the scene I'd ended up choosing from the play, which was a dialogue between Cinderella and one of her stepsisters. Usually, when I practiced, I had someone else read the stepsister's part. But since I didn't have anyone to help me read onstage, I read the lines of both characters, going back and forth between the two. It

felt a little strange, but by the end, I was having fun, and Ms. Kamper and the other people in the audience laughed too!

"Excellent!" Ms. Kamper exclaimed when I was done. "Good job, Mindy!"

She had a gleam in her eyes, like she was very excited.

I hoped this meant I was going to get good news soon!

Chapter 6

Time seemed to be moving slower than a snail for the next few days while we waited for the audition results. Part of me wanted to know right away, but the other part hoped we would never find out who got what role. I was so afraid that I wouldn't make it into the musical!

The day before the announcement, Dad found me lying on my bed with Theodore while staring up at the ceiling.

Theodore wagged his tail when Dad came over to sit with us.

"Mindy, are you okay?" he asked.

"Yeah . . . ," I said. "I'm just nervous about tomorrow. We're supposed to find out about the summer musical!"

"Right," he replied. "And how are you feeling about that?"

"It's exciting!" I exclaimed. "But it's also scary. What if Lindsey and Sally get in and I don't?"

Dad sat next to me on the bed. "I know neither of us knows the results yet, but I *do* know for sure that you tried your best. And that's all that matters, okay?"

I nodded. Dad was right. I *did* do my best! Besides, it wasn't like I could time-travel and redo my audition. Although that would be really cool if I could!

The next morning, Dad was on his tablet when he suddenly yelled, "Mindy! Julie! Come quick! I got the e-mail with the cast announcement!"

We all gathered in the living room. Theodore came running too. He didn't know what was happening, but he wagged his tail and ran in circles.

He looked just as excited as we all were!

Dad glanced at me before he opened the e-mail. "Are you ready?"

I nodded. "Yes!"

He tapped the screen. Julie and I peered over his shoulders so we could see, too.

The e-mail said: *Congratulations! Your daughter, Mindy Kim, has been cast for the role of . . .*

"*An evil stepsister?*" I gasped, putting my hands to my face.

Dad scratched his head, looking very puzzled.

"Huh," he said. "Didn't see that one coming. But congrats, Mindy! That's one of the bigger supporting roles. You made it into the play!"

"But I didn't even try out for that role!" I yelled. "Why did they cast me for it?"

I was sad. I wondered why they thought I would be a good evil stepsister. Did I accidentally seem mean in my audition? What if this meant I would be a bad sister to my new baby sibling?

I tried my best not to cry. Good or not, I was going to be a big sister soon! I didn't want to cry like a baby anymore.

"Now, now, I'm sure they chose you for that role for a good reason!" Dad said. "Maybe Ms. Kamper liked how you read the lines for the stepsister better than Cinderella's during your audition. You *were* good at both characters. If you want me to, I can e-mail Ms. Kamper and ask about the decision."

I shook my head. I was too afraid to find out the truth. Instead, I asked Dad if I could use his tablet to call Sally and Lindsey. Both my friends picked up almost immediately. Sally looked like she'd been crying, while there was a bright smile on Lindsey's face. Lindsey stopped grinning when she saw the looks on our faces.

"Oh no!" she said. "Did you two not make it into the musical?"

"I got cast as one of the evil stepsisters!" I exclaimed, unable to keep it in any longer. "I don't know how I feel about it, since I auditioned for Cinderella, *not* a mean sister."

"I got cast as an evil stepsister too!" Sally exclaimed, looking relieved. "Whew! I was so mad when I first found out, but hearing that you're the other one makes me feel a lot better. Maybe this musical won't be so bad after all!"

We both looked at Lindsey, who gave us a nervous laugh. "Um. Well . . . I got cast as Cinderella! But I'm sure you two deserved the role too! I–"

"No, you completely deserved it." Sally said. "You were definitely better than both of us. You made Ms. Kamper cry!"

"Yup, you totally did," I agreed. "Even though I'm sad I didn't get cast as Cinderella, I'm so glad you got the role!"

"Same," Sally replied.

Lindsey gave us a shy smile. "Aw, thanks, guys."

"Honestly," Sally continued, "I'm so glad that we all made it into the play! It could have been a lot worse."

"That's so true!" I looked at my friends' faces on Dad's tablet and smiled.

Even though things didn't turn out the way we thought they would, I was glad that at least all three of us were going to be in the summer musical!

Chapter 7

The more I thought about being cast as an evil stepsister, the more it bothered me. Later that night, when Dad came into my room to tuck me in, I got into my bed with a heavy sigh.

"What's wrong, Mindy?" he asked. "Is everything okay?"

"Yup," I said, trying to give him a big smile. "My friends and I all got roles in *Cinderella*!"

"Right," Dad said. "But . . . you don't look too happy about it. Not anymore, at least. Is there something else that's bothering you?"

I sighed again and told Dad the truth. Or at least

part of it. I couldn't let Dad and Julie know that I already had doubts about being a good sister!

"It still bothers me that I got cast as an evil stepsister. I know I'm lucky enough to even have a role, but . . . evil stepsister? Does this mean I look like a bad kid?"

"Hm . . . let me see. . . ."

Dad furrowed his eyebrows and stared intently at my face with a pretend magnifying glass as if searching for clues.

I squeezed my eyes shut, bracing myself. Maybe I did look mean after all!

After only a couple of seconds, though, Dad laughed. "Oh, Mindy, I'm just kidding. Of course you don't look like a bad kid!"

"But something about me must have made the teacher cast me as a stepsister! And not one of the mice or something else."

Dad shrugs. "Maybe you were just good enough to get a major supporting role, and this evil stepsister was the one that fit you the most in terms of singing range! Besides, people who play evil characters aren't actually bad in real life. They're just great actors! You also made Ms. Kamper laugh when you read your scene, remember? The stepsisters are supposed to be the comic relief, which means they're in the play to make everyone laugh. Maybe that kind of character was just a better fit for you!"

I rested my head on my hands and thought carefully about what Dad had said. A lot of people *did* laugh when I read lines from my scene.

"Maybe!" I finally replied.

"Being an evil stepsister isn't necessarily a bad thing, Mindy," Dad said with a grin. "It doesn't have as much responsibility as a lead role like Cinderella, and you can also have a lot more fun with it! I always thought the evil stepsisters were the funniest part of the play. Making people laugh is an important thing to do!"

"But everyone hates the evil stepsisters," I said.

"Most people probably do, but just because people hate someone doesn't mean they're really bad. Sometimes it means that the person is their own self instead of just being who everyone thinks they should be. Like Princess Pyeonggang!"

"Princess Pyeonggang?" I asked. The name sounded familiar, but I couldn't remember who that was.

Dad went to my bookshelf and got out the book of old Korean folk tales that my mom gave me when I was little.

"Yes! From this story over here."

He flipped to the story about Princess Pyeonggang and Ondal.

"Oh, I remember now!" I exclaimed. "Pyeonggang is the princess who people made fun of because she cried too much! But even then she was still able to help her husband, Ondal, become an awesome general!"

Dad smiled. "Yup, that's exactly it! She wasn't an evil stepsister, but a lot of people didn't like the princess because she cried a lot and didn't always behave the way people thought she should. But she still stood up for herself and became a heroine in her own right. And Ondal, who everyone thought was the village fool, ended up becoming a great general, too, despite what people thought of him."

Dad closed the book and pulled me into a hug.

"Just because other people might think someone is bad, it doesn't mean they really are, Mindy. Plus, even as an evil stepsister, *you* can still be your best self, make people laugh, and help others. Always remember that!"

"Okay," I said, giving Dad a kiss on the cheek. "Thanks, Appa."

I felt a lot better by the time I fell asleep.

Chapter 8

When everyone arrived at the theater for our first rehearsal, Ms. Kamper said, "Congratulations to all of you for making it into the musical! The competition was fierce this year, and the audition was not easy, so you all should be proud of yourselves."

My friends and I shared a smile. We were definitely proud of ourselves!

"Today we're going to run through the whole play with our scripts, just so everyone can get a sense of what the play is like when we're all together onstage," Ms. Kamper continued. "But remember that we are not going to use the scripts for the actual play. So please work hard to memorize your lines by our dress rehearsal at the end of the month."

I stared down at the script in my hands. Suddenly I was glad I didn't have that many lines to memorize. Beside me, Lindsey gulped. I didn't blame her. She had so many lines to learn!

When it was her turn, Lindsey had a hard time reading her lines. Her voice was shaky and came out in short stutters. "I–I–"

"Wow, how did she become Cinderella if she's so bad?" whispered Kyle, the boy who was supposed to be Prince Charming.

I gave him a stink eye. "She's just nervous!" I exclaimed. "She was really good at the actual audition."

"Sure, sure, whatever you say, evil stepsister!" replied Kyle.

I gasped. Before he spoke, I'd thought he looked every bit as handsome as a prince. But now I wasn't so sure!

"Kyle, that's enough, please," Ms. Kamper said before she turned back to Lindsey. She gave her a patient smile. "It's okay, Lindsey. Being the lead always comes with a lot of pressure. You just have to work your way through it. Let's try that again."

But no matter how many times Lindsey tried, she only seemed to get worse. Finally, tears started coming out of her eyes. Some of the girls who'd also tried out for Cinderella looked annoyed. I couldn't read minds, but I could tell they were wondering why she was cast as Cinderella and not them!

I thought about what Dad said about how I could still help people even though I was cast as an evil stepsister. I shared a look with Sally.

"We have to get her out of here, quick!" I whispered.

Sally nodded, and we both raised our hands.

Ms. Kamper called on me, and I asked, "Can Sally and I help our friend Lindsey? I think she just needs a little pep talk!"

Ms. Kamper looked a bit confused, but she still smiled and replied, "Sure, Mindy! Why don't we all take a ten-minute break? Please let me know if there's anything I can do to help."

I held one of Lindsey's hands while Sally held the other. Together we went to the backstage area.

"Sorry," Lindsey said when the three of us were alone. "I think I'm too nervous. I'll practice my lines a lot and be super good, I promise!"

"It's okay—we all get a little bit of stage fright sometimes," Sally replied. "My mom taught me a special way to calm down when I feel nervous. Want me to show you how?"

Lindsey and I both exclaimed, "Sure!"

I *definitely* wanted to know Sally's secret technique!

"Well, what you do is count to four when you breathe in . . ."

We each took a breath.

"Hold for seven seconds . . ."

I did my best to hold my breath. Seven seconds seemed to take forever!

"And then let out the breath for eight seconds!" Sally finished. "I usually feel a lot better afterward."

Lindsey and I did what Sally said, letting our breath out in slow puffs of air. By the end, my head felt a little light, but in a good way. And I felt relaxed!

"Wow, that helped a lot!" Lindsey said. "I feel much better already."

"It's like magic!" I added.

Sally grinned. "It's a neat trick, for sure!"

I turned to Lindsey, thinking about what my dad had said about being the main character. "Being Cinderella is a lot of hard work and pressure, but I believe in you! You were so good at the audition! Sally and I are here to cheer you on."

"Yup, I believe in you too!" Sally said. "Evil or not, we're still your stepsisters."

She winked at Lindsey, and we all laughed.

Just then, a boy with round brown eyes joined us backstage.

"Hey!" he said. "Are you okay, Lindsey? Sorry about Kyle. He's a big bully at my school, so I was disappointed when he got cast as the prince. I didn't even know he liked theater! He probably just wants to be the star."

"If he's a bully, then why is he the prince?" Sally asked, sounding confused. I was curious too. How could something like this have happened?

The boy shrugged. "He's tall and good at singing!

And he didn't mess up during the audition like I did. I tried out too, but my nerves got the best of me, and I got cast as a mouse instead, even though I practiced all the lines for the prince."

"That stinks!" Lindsey exclaimed. "Sorry . . . what's your name again?"

"Tim," the boy said. "Anyway, I'm glad you're okay now. If you three ever need help standing up against Kyle, let me know!"

He gave us all a big smile, looking a lot more like Prince Charming than Kyle ever could.

Chapter 9

A couple of weeks later, I got a call from Lindsey.

"I can't memorize my lines no matter how hard I try!" she cried.

Thanks to Julie's and Dad's help, I'd already memorized my lines, but I had a lot fewer scenes than Lindsey.

"Did you ask your parents for help?" I asked. "Dad and Julie have been helping me with my lines."

"My dad's back in Minnesota, with my other grandparents, and my mom's busy with work. Usually I can ask my grandma—my mom's mom—but she's got her hands full right now with my brother.

He's having a hard time with summer school, so she's been busy trying to figure that out."

I frowned. What could I do? Then I got an idea.

After Lindsey and I hung up, I called Sally. "Are you free this weekend?"

"Uh . . . not on Sunday, but I should be free on Saturday!"

"Perfect!" I said. "We should help Lindsey memorize her lines and practice our lines all together, just like we did before the audition!"

"Okay! Maybe we can make it into a fun beach day, too, since Lindsey's house is by the beach!"

"That's an awesome idea!"

On Saturday, we met up in our bathing suits at the beach by Lindsey's house. Since Lindsey's mom was at work and Lindsey's grandma was busy helping her brother with summer school homework, Dad, Julie, and Sally's parents came to the beach with us.

Dad and Mr. Johnson set up big umbrellas

and lawn chairs so we could stay by the beach for as long as we wanted. Once we were settled, we opened up our baskets of snacks! Happily munching away on shrimp chips and Pepero and enjoying the ocean breeze, Sally, Lindsey, and I went over our lines together.

After a while, Dad said, "Hey, Mindy, can we help you kids practice, too?"

"Sure!" I said. "The more the merrier!"

There were more roles in the play than adults, so everyone picked and chose multiple. Dad read the lines of both the prince and the mice, Julie read the lines of the stepmother and the fairy godmother, and Sally's parents read everything else. It was our own family production!

We stayed there until sunset going over the script, taking breaks to swim in the water and build sandcastles. We even made up our own play where all three of us could be princesses!

"And they all lived happily ever after!" Sally

exclaimed at the end. "See? We don't need princes! We can just rescue each other."

"Yeah!" Lindsey and I exclaimed.

We gave each other a high five.

Chapter 10

The next rehearsal felt way more like the real play now that more of us knew our lines. Instead of just staring at our scripts the whole time, we could look at one another and more freely move around the stage!

I didn't have many lines as an evil stepsister, and the ones I did have weren't very nice. It felt weird to say mean things, but then I remembered what Dad had said about how I could still try my best to make people laugh.

"Cinderella, wash my dress!" said Sally as the other stepsister. She held her nose high up in the air.

In a very squeaky voice, I said, "Cinderella, style my hair!"

Sally giggled, but everyone else looked confused. Ms. Kamper coughed but didn't say anything.

When we had to sing about how we were so excited about the ball, I saw another chance to make people laugh. Instead of just singing normally, I held Sally's hand and wiggled from head to toe as I sang.

More people laughed this time, including Tim, who was watching us from where he was waiting for his scene at the back of the stage. Our eyes met, and he gave me a thumbs-up.

"Mindy?" Ms. Kamper asked. "Could I please speak with you for a moment, please? Everyone, let's take a ten-minute break."

I gulped and followed Ms. Kamper to the back of the stage. She had a big frown on her face. By the time I reached her, I was super nervous.

"I'm so sorry, Ms. Kamper!" I blurted out before she could say anything. "My dad told me I should make the best of being an evil stepsister, so I was just trying to be funny. I didn't mean to be a bad actress!"

I held my breath as I waited for Ms. Kamper's response. Thankfully, she smiled.

"Ah, so that's what you were doing!" she exclaimed. "I was afraid you weren't taking the play seriously, but it seems like you were doing the opposite. I love that you're trying to be more creative with the role, Mindy!"

"Really?" I beamed.

She nodded. "Yup! Sure, your comedic timing and improv skills *could* use some more work, but that's why we're practicing, right? Does Sally also know what you're up to?"

I slapped my forehead. I'd totally forgotten to tell her!

Ms. Kamper laughed. "I'll take that as a sign that

you haven't. Why don't you tell Sally what you're try-ing to do? If the two of you plan things out together, it'll make everything even better."

"Okay!" I exclaimed.

The play just got a lot more fun!

Chapter 11

Sally and I practiced our lines together, silly parts and all. We checked with Lindsey, our families, and even our dogs to see what was and wasn't funny!

Soon it was time for our dress rehearsal. It was so fun seeing everyone in their costumes. Sally and I both had dresses with fun, puffy sleeves and bows on our heads, while Lindsey had a simple cleaning dress for most of the scenes and a fancy light blue gown for the ball. My favorite costumes were for the kids who played the mice. Each costume had big, floppy ears and a round black nose, just like a real mouse. They were so cute!

Everyone loved Sally's and my funny moments, and things were going well up until the very end of the rehearsal, when Lindsey forgot one of her lines.

"I–" she started and stopped. "I . . ."

Everyone gawked and stared. And then Kyle laughed. "Oh man, I can't believe she messed up that line!"

"Hey!" I yelled. "Lindsey worked hard to learn her lines."

"Yeah!" Sally joined in. "It's just one mistake."

I was about to say something else when Tim stepped forward, mouse costume and all.

"Aren't you supposed to be Prince Charming?" he asked Kyle. "You've been nothing but mean to her ever since the first rehearsal. That's not really a princelike thing to do."

The other kids chimed in, saying similar things.

I folded my arms, and we all stared him down. Kyle glanced around at all of us and then at Ms.

Kamper, who also looked disappointed in him. I thought he was going to say sorry, but instead he made a grouchy face and said, "I quit!"

He stormed off.

Ms. Kamper gasped. She held her head in her hands. "That was our prince! What are we going to do now? The play is next week!"

No one said anything for the longest time. But then I raised my hand.

"I know who can be our new prince!" I pointed at Tim. "Tim knows all the lines, and unlike Kyle, he's super nice! He should be our real prince."

When Ms. Kamper turned to look at him, Tim nodded and said, "I know the songs, too. Even though I didn't get the part when I auditioned, I still really liked the prince's part of the play, so I kept practicing his stuff since I only had a couple of lines as the mouse."

Ms. Kamper thought about it and said, "Okay,

Tim, do you feel up for the challenge? Unfortunately, we don't have much time since the play is next week. It's clear from today that Kyle isn't well-suited for the role anyway, so I'd much rather you have it if you're sure you're up to it."

"Yeah!" Tim said. "I was nervous when I auditioned, so I messed up, but I feel more confident now that I've practiced a lot more. I'm still scared, though—is that okay?"

"Of course!" Ms. Kamper replied. "Even the best performers on Broadway still get scared sometimes. You just have to keep working your way through it."

Tim nodded. "Okay, I can do that."

"Great! It's official, then," Ms. Kamper announced. "Tim is our new prince! We'll have to get you fitted for the prince costume as soon as possible, but it can be done."

Everyone cheered, and Lindsey looked relieved

most of all. I was proud of Sally, Tim, and me for standing up for her, and happy that Tim got the role he deserved.

Dad was right. Maybe being an evil stepsister wasn't so bad after all!

Chapter 12

Finally, it was the day of the play!

I put on my dress, and Julie helped me put on stage makeup. Ms. Kamper recommended that every kid put on makeup for the play because the strong lights could make people look like ghosts.

I closed my eyes and stayed as still as I could as Julie put makeup on my face. It smelled nice, but my face felt heavy, like I was wearing a mask. I'd tried on lipstick and blush a few times, but this was my first time getting a full face of makeup!

I felt a little warm, so I wasn't too sure about the whole makeup thing. I was about to ask Julie if she

63

could take everything off when she turned my seat around so I could look in the bathroom mirror.

"You can open your eyes now, Mindy!" she said.

"Wow, I look like a completely different person!" I exclaimed.

My lips were bright red, and my eyelids were painted a pretty blue. Julie had even put eyeliner that curled up on the edges around my eyes. I definitely looked like an evil stepsister now!

Dad clapped his hands and laughed when he saw my face. "That's perfect! Good job, Julie!"

"Yeah, it looks awesome!" I agreed.

Julie smiled and gave a little bow. "Thank you! I did my best."

When we were all ready, Dad, Julie, and I went to the community theater. I said hi to all my friends, who also had on makeup and their costumes. Everyone looked so good! I was really excited to see how everything would turn out.

Dad and Julie gave me one last hug before I had to go backstage.

"Break a leg!" Dad said.

I wrinkled my nose and smiled. Even though I knew it was just a saying, I still thought it sounded funny. "Thanks, Appa!"

Backstage, everyone was panicking. The kids playing the mice were running around screaming. The fairy godmother was fighting with the queen. Tim was anxiously staring down at the script.

I found Sally peering out at the audience through the edge of the curtain. "I can see my sisters and parents from here!" she said. "And look, Mindy, there's your dad and Julie!"

I looked through from behind the curtain too. Julie and Dad had just found their seats beside Sally's and Lindsey's families. I bit my lip. I hoped I could make them proud today!

Ms. Kamper came running backstage and clapped her hands. Her hair looked messier than usual, and her glasses were tilted.

"Everyone!" she exclaimed. "Please gather around. We'll do one last huddle before we begin."

We all went quiet as we did what she said.

"No matter what happens today, I just wanted to say that I'm so proud of everyone," Ms. Kamper said. "You all worked hard! You should be proud of *yourselves*, too. And remember, it's okay to make mistakes! The most important thing is to gracefully move on from them and do better next time. Let's put on the best show we can and have fun, okay?"

"Yeah!" We all cheered.

Everyone got into their places onstage and waited for the curtains to go up. I squeezed Sally's and Lindsey's hands. They squeezed my hands back.

"We can do this!" I said. "Let's break our legs!"

Lindsey and Sally laughed.

"That sounds so funny," Sally said. "But yeah, let's try our best!"

We let go of one another as the curtain went up.

Chapter 13

The audience burst into loud applause as we began the opening song about the upcoming ball. The stage lights felt hot on my skin, and I was already getting sweaty, but I couldn't keep the grin off my face as I sang. All together, we sounded so good! And I was so happy to be part of the group. Even though being onstage alone was still scary, being onstage with everyone else was so fun.

Lindsey was the perfect Cinderella, her voice clear and pretty like a songbird's as she sang. When it was time for us to get ready for the ball, Sally and I pretended to fight each other, and everyone laughed. I had to try really hard to not giggle. I loved making other people laugh!

We were almost done with the scene when something horrible happened. Lindsey forgot one of her lines!

Her eyes wide with panic, she stood frozen onstage.

Luckily, I knew what came next! I whispered the line to her, and she said it right away. Everyone let out a sigh of relief.

"Thanks, Mindy!" she whispered to me as we moved on to the next scene.

The set for the ball was so pretty, like we were in a real castle! Tim and Lindsey looked so good together as they danced onstage. It was hard try- ing to act like I was angry at the two of them during the entire scene.

Finally, it was time for the three of us to try

Cinderella's slipper. Sally was so funny, huffing and puffing as she tried to make the shoe fit. The audience laughed. I hoped I could make everyone laugh too!

When it was my turn to try on the slipper, I screamed and swung my leg around, causing the shoe to go flying. It was something I'd practiced, but I must have kicked too hard this time!

From backstage, Ms. Kamper gasped, and Tim ran across the stage to get the shoe.

"Oops!" I said.

I felt bad, but everyone laughed so much I smiled too.

Operation Make People Laugh was a success!

When the shoe fit Lindsey, and she and Tim had their happy ending, I hid my mouth with my hands so no one could see me grin. It was such a cute moment!

The audience cheered loudly for us at the end, and some people even got up to give us a standing

ovation! We all stood at the front of the stage and held hands. I held Sally's hand on my right and Lindsey's on my left as we bowed.

We'd done it! We'd finished the musical!

Chapter 14

In the theater lobby, Dad and Julie greeted me with a big bouquet of flowers.

"Congratulations, Mindy!" exclaimed Dad. "You were amazing!"

"Yes, congratulations!" Julie added. "We're both so proud of you. You were such a funny evil stepsister!"

They both gave me a big hug. Around me, everyone else's families and friends were hugging them, too.

"Whew, I'm glad!" I replied. "I was trying my hardest to make everyone laugh. And . . ."

I paused, wondering if I should finally tell Dad and Julie the whole truth.

"What is it, Mindy?" Dad asked.

He and Julie both looked worried as they stared at me.

I sighed, and, after making sure no one around us was looking, I whispered, "I was nervous about being cast as an evil stepsister because I thought that meant that I was going to be a bad sister in real life!"

Julie laughed, covering her mouth with her hands. "Oh, Mindy. You can't possibly be a bad sister. Just look at what a good friend you are!"

"That's right," Dad agreed. "Being a good friend isn't that much different from being a good sibling. Sure, you three aren't related by blood, but aren't you, Sally, and Lindsey all sisters in a way?"

I glanced at where Sally and Lindsey were with their families. Dad was right! Sally and I had even joked that we were like Lindsey's real stepsisters.

My friends looked so happy, and I was glad we all had fun in the musical.

"Just like you girls helped one another through this new experience, the three of us can also set off on this brand-new adventure one day at a time," Julie said. "We're all in this together, okay? So you don't have to put so much pressure on yourself, Mindy."

"Okay," I replied. I was crying, not because I was sad, but because I was happy and so excited for the future.

We came together again in a big, happy hug.

Acknowledgments

It's somehow a brand-new year of Mindy Kim books! When I first thought of writing Mindy's story in 2018, I could never have imagined that I would still be writing her books five years later. This is all thanks to you, reader, and the countless others who have made this series possible. Every student, parent, teacher, librarian, and bookseller who has read and shared Mindy's stories . . . thank you, from the bottom of my heart, for being Mindy's friend.

Special thanks goes to my editor, Alyson Heller, and my illustrator, Dung Ho. The Mindy Kim books simply *would not be* the Mindy Kim books without either of them. I just provide the words, and they bring them to life. Thank you also to Laura Lyn DiSiena and everyone else who's helped make the

Mindy books as humanly cute as possible since Day One. Every day I feel so incredibly blessed to have such a fantastic team for this series.

Additionally, thank you to the many teachers who guided me and my classmates through musicals, concerts, and plays while I was in school. And of course, thank you also to my parents, who attended every such event that filled up my childhood and helped me practice for all those years.

I say this often but that's because it's true: being a writer would be an incredibly lonely experience without friends, and I'm fortunate to have Amelie Wen Zhao, Katie Zhao, Aneeqah Naeem, Bernice Yau, Francesca Flores, Huihua He, Hester Lee, Rey Noble, Margaret Zeng, Chloe Gong, Annie Lee, Linh Truong, Irene Yen, Stephanie Lu, Kaiti Liu, Angelica Tran, Chelsea Chang, Luke Chou, Kris Wong, Alice Zhu, and many others who brighten up my life. I am so grateful for all of you!

Don't miss

♥ **Mindy's** ♥

next adventure!

My name is Mindy Kim, and today started like any other day. I got up from bed, and my dog, Theodore the Mutt, wagged his tail and yawned. The sound he made was so cute!

"Good morning, Theodore!" I said, and patted him on the head.

I went to the bathroom like I always did in the morning. As I was in there, I heard the phone ring.

When I came out, though, it was quiet. Usually, either Dad or my stepmom, Julie, is already up. But this morning, no one was there in the hallway to say, "Good morning, Mindy!"

Holding my breath, I walked over to my parents' bedroom door and leaned against the door. Dad and Julie were whispering in their room. I couldn't hear exactly what they were saying, but I could tell it wasn't anything good.

I bit my lip and looked at the doorknob. I wasn't sure if I should open the door or not! I looked down at Theodore, who wagged his tail again, but more slowly this time. He looked like he was encouraging me, so I reached out and opened the door.

Dad was sitting on his bed, clutching his phone with both hands. He was turned away from me, so I couldn't see his face, but his shoulders were shaking. Was he crying?

Julie stood beside him with her hand resting on his shoulder.

"What's wrong, Appa?" I asked softly, saying the Korean word for "Daddy."

Dad turned to look at me but just shook his head. Julie took me by the hand and led me out of the room.

After closing the door behind us, she gently placed her hands on my shoulders, took a deep breath, and said, "We got bad news from Korea, Mindy. Your grandfather passed away. We just found out. I'm so sorry."

My heart dropped to my feet. Just last week I'd called my grandpa and grandma. They'd both seemed so healthy and happy!

"But how?" I asked. My voice came out quiet and small. "Was there an accident?"

Julie shook her head. "Thankfully not, but sometimes people your grandpa's age die suddenly. The doctor said it was a heart attack."

Tears welled up in my eyes, but I wiped them away as soon as Dad came out of the room. I didn't want him to see me cry! Grandpa was his dad, so I couldn't even imagine how sad he was. Seeing me cry would only make him even sadder.

He reached toward us, and Julie and I hugged him tight. We stayed there for a while, holding him steady as he shook from head to toe.

"Mindy," Dad said. "Could you please go to your room for a bit? I have to talk to Julie about something. Don't worry about school today. We'll call and tell them there's been a family emergency."

I went back in my room with Theodore and waited. When we'd first found out Julie was pregnant, I put my stuffed animals in a box to give to my younger sibling when they were born. But the baby wasn't here yet, and I needed my plushies more than ever. I got the box out of the closet and hugged Mr. Toe Beans, my stuffed corgi, tight.

Theodore whimpered, so I made sure to give him a hug too.

After a while, Dad and Julie came into my room. Dad still looked sad, but he wasn't crying anymore.

"Mindy, we've decided to go to Korea for the funeral," he said. "Chuseok is around the corner, and since it's an important holiday in Korea, like Thanksgiving is in America, I think we're all better off spending some time with our family right now."

In the US, my family doesn't usually celebrate Chuseok, so I wasn't sure what to expect. During this time of year, we just eat *songpyeon*–sweet rice cakes shaped like crescent moons–and moon cakes. Songpyeon are what Koreans like Dad and me eat for Chuseok, while moon cakes are what Chinese people like Julie and her family eat for the Mid-Autumn Festival.

"How long will we be in Korea?" I asked.

The last time we visited, it was during the summer. I doubted we could stay in Korea for as long as we did then, but I hoped we could still spend lots of time with our relatives during this trip too.

"Probably just a week," Dad said, talking really fast. He almost sounded like a robot! "Unfortunately, Julie and I can't get more time off work, and since you still have school . . .that's the best we can do. We have to get to the Atlanta airport by this evening for our flight to Korea in order to make it in time for the funeral, so we need to hurry and pack. We can ask Eunice to come check on Theodore while we are gone."

"Before we do, though . . ." Julie pulled Dad and me into another big hug. "Let's take deep breaths. I love both of you very much. I'm here for you, okay?"

Dad breathed in slowly and gave Julie a kiss on the forehead. I buried my head deep into Julie's arms, pulling both her and Dad in for a big group hug.

I was still sad about Grandpa, but I was also happy we were going to Korea again. After our last trip, I hadn't been sure when we would next visit. I'd also never been to a funeral *or* celebrated a holiday in Korea before, so I didn't know what to expect. I didn't even know if we could make it in time for our flight!

I packed my bags, hoping everything would all work out.

About the Author

Lyla Lee is the author of the Mindy Kim series, as well as *I'll Be the One* and *Flip the Script* for teens. Born in South Korea, she's since then lived in various parts of the United States, including California, Florida, and Texas. Inspired by her English teacher, she started writing her own stories in fourth grade and finished her first novel at the age of fourteen. After working in Hollywood and studying psychology and cinematic arts at the University of Southern California, she now lives in Dallas, Texas. You can visit her online at lylaleebooks.com.